# PALACE PUPPIES

PREVIOUSLY IN THE
# PALACE PUPPIES
SERIES

## Sunny and the Royal Party

# PALACE PUPPIES

## Sunny to the Rescue

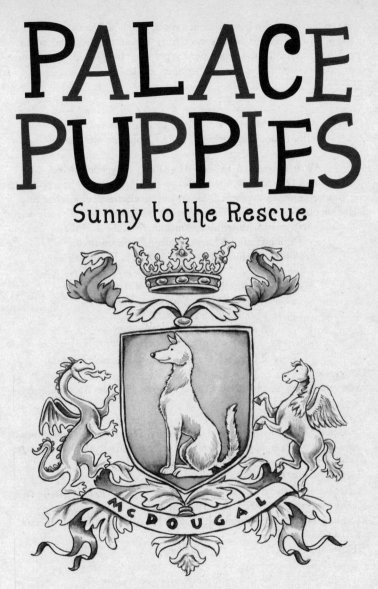

MCDOUGAL

By Laura Dower
Illustrated by John Steven Gurney

DISNEP • HYPERION BOOKS
NEW YORK

Text copyright © 2013 by Laura Dower
Illustrations copyright © 2013 by John Steven Gurney

Printed in the United States of America
First Edition
10 9 8 7 6 5 4 3 2 1
J689-1817-1-13105

Library of Congress Cataloging-in-Publication Data
Dower, Laura.
Sunny to the rescue / by Laura Dower; illustrated by John Steven Gurney.—1st ed.
p. cm.—(Palace puppies; bk. 2)
Summary: Spending the day at the beach with Princess Annie and Prince James, royal puppy Sunny, a well-behaved goldendoodle, comes to the rescue when her mischievous companion, Rex the beagle, goes missing.
ISBN 978-1-4231-6486-9
[1. Behavior—Fiction. 2. Beaches—Fiction. 3. Lost and found possessions—Fiction. 4. Dogs—Fiction. 5. Animals—Infancy—Fiction. 6. Princes—Fiction. 7. Princesses—Fiction.] I. Gurney, John Steven, 1962– ill. II. Title.
PZ7.D75458Sv 2013
[Fic]—dc23                    2012020300

Visit www.disneyhyperionbooks.com

For Golden Emma and
Chocolate Charlie
and their masters:
Matthew, Gjon, and Lucas

# Chapter 1

"It's too hot to play, Rex!" I yelped.

Outside, the temperature was headed toward the triple digits. Inside, the palace air conditioner was busted. There was no escape from the heat. I thought it was a good idea to stay as still as possible.

Rex, on the other hand, wanted to run and play and chase his tail in a circle.

*Pant, pant, pant. Huff, huff, huff.*

"It's so hot, Rex! Please stop that racket!" I begged.

"Racket?" Rex pushed his ears *waaay* back. "Who said anything about tennis?"

He darted past me and flew across the room.

"Aw, Rex! All that running around is making me hotter," I grumbled, shaking my golden head. "Royal puppies should know how to keep their cool."

I knew Rex was a good doggy, deep down. But sometimes I wished that that royal beagle had an off button.

If only Annie had been right there right now, covering me with a wet cloth, pouring me a bowl of ice-cold water, and tossing me a Snappy Snap. No, a *fistful* of Snappy Snaps! She knew how to make everything better.

Annie was the princess of McDougal Palace. I belonged to her. Annie's brother, James, was the prince. James took care of Rex. We all lived there together in the palace with King Jon and Queen Katherine and a whole staff of nannies, chefs, gardeners, and butlers.

Rex and I have called the castle home ever since we were wee pups. We usually got along even though we were so different. After all, we got everything we needed there. Annie gave me lots of attention and scratched behind my ears in just the right spots. Rex and I knew we were lucky to live in a place where the supply of dog toys never ran out and there was an adventure behind every royal door.

"*Aaaaaaaaaaarf!*" Rex nuzzled my side and jumped up into the air like he had springs on his paws. Then he took off and zoomed around me again, nearly colliding with a door frame.

I felt dizzy watching him spin. He nearly bumped into an umbrella stand.

"Rex!" I called out. "Slow down!"

"Rowf!" Rex just barked back at me, with a toss of his head. He didn't mind the heat, and he definitely wasn't ready to stay still. That dog wiggled and waggled, and then his tail flipped so hard that it knocked a folded newspaper off the hall table.

The paper fell to the floor with a thud.

"Now look what you've done! That paper probably belongs to King Jon!" I cried. "Quick, let's put it back."

Rex snatched the paper into his mouth, and I thought he would put it back on the table. But instead he dropped it at my feet. As it fell open, I saw the headline on the front page.

"Read it! Read it!" Rex panted.

# Glimmer Rock Gazette

## IT'S A ROYAL HEAT WAVE!
## ONE HUNDRED DEGREES IN THE SHADE

GLIMMER ROCK
IS HOT!

Temperatures are expected to reach the 100-degree mark today in the kingdom of Glimmer Rock. If you are headed to the beach, be sure to bring plenty of sunscreen and drinking water.

An oversized photograph showed a crowded beachfront dotted with colorful umbrellas and packed with people. In the distance was the enormous "rock" of Glimmer Rock, sparkling in the sun like a massive diamond. Everyone was lying out on towels and beach chairs at the foot of the rock. There were dogs there, too.

The kingdom of Glimmer Rock had pet-friendly beaches. Actually, the kingdom of Glimmer Rock had pet-friendly *everything*.

Oh, how I loved Glimmer Rock Beach!

Looking at the photograph, I could almost smell the warm sea breezes. It brought back a rush of wonderful memories. When I was a teeny-tiny new puppy, Annie, James, and the king and queen took me to that beach for the very first time.

I remember Annie carrying me to Glimmer Rock in a little brown basket. She made me wear a hat on my soft puppy head and little cotton booties to cover my delicate paws, so I wouldn't get sunburned. She slathered goopy coconut lotion onto my snout, too. I remember licking it off, thinking it would taste like sugar frosting.

*Blecch!* It wasn't delicious at all.

Annie and James took me to the beach a lot

during my first year at the palace. I would watch them build sand castles while I dug the moats. My enormous puppy paws were good for digging trenches in the sand. After we built our castle, we'd sit there and wait for the ocean to sweep it up and wash it away.

When we weren't building castles, I'd chase sandpipers in the surf and sniff crabs out of their holes. Getting wet was the best part. Even though the salt water stung my puppy eyes sometimes, I loved diving into waves. James liked to splash me, too.

I was a regular beach doodle!

But that was before Rex arrived at the palace.

Once James got Rex, we stopped going to the beach. Annie told me once that the king and queen worried that bringing two dogs to Glimmer Rock Beach would be too much trouble. So I forgot about the sandpipers and the crabs. I forgot about the sand-castle moats.

Until now.

Now, in the midst of this incredible heat wave, I remembered it all. I wanted to be on that beach again.

*"ROWF!"*

I barked for Annie. I had to tell her what I was thinking. If it was too hot to stay inside like this, then we needed to go to the beach. Two dogs would be twice the fun! Of course, I'd mind my manners. And I would help keep an eye on wild Rex. We could build the biggest and best sand castle ever— together!

"*ROWF!*" I barked again. Still no one answered.

Where was my princess? Was she playing a game of hide-and-seek?

As I scampered across the entrance hall in search of Annie, my nails click-clacked on the floor. The palace entryway had been retiled in dark pink marble. The floor was cool, like I imagined a skating rink would be. I'd seen the way ice skaters glided across the ice, twirling and twisting as if someone were pulling them on a string.

Could these tiles cool me off? I lay down and pressed my belly to the marble.

*Aaaaaah.*

It worked!

The chilly tiles made me forget instantly about the heat. I began to daydream about sweet ocean breezes and cool beach water lapping against my overheated fur. I could take to the ocean like a champ, too. Goldendoodles are natural-born swimmers! It's no secret that my best stroke is the doggy paddle.

I must have been there for a few moments, stretched out on the tiles daydreaming about the beach, when out of nowhere, Rex pounced onto my back. He thought he was being funny, but I was *not* amused. Then Rex began to sniff around my head.

Honestly, that dog was drooling on my coat!

"What are you doing ?" I barked.

"What am I doing? What are *you* doing?" Rex asked. "You can't just lie there on the floor, Sunny. Get up and play!"

"Rex, can't you see? I'm not playing right now; I'm just daydreaming," I said. "You try it. Let the tiles cool off your thoughts. . . ."

Rex tilted his head to one side. "Fine," he grumbled. "I'll *try*."

Slowly, he slid down onto his belly. I was sure he'd cool off. But as soon his tummy hit the floor, Rex jumped right back up.

"Zowie! That tickles!" he yelped. "I don't want to lie down anyway. I want to play! Play!"

8

"No!" I barked a second time. "I told you I don't want to play!"

Rex's whole head sank down. He stared at me and then at the floor. He slunk away in the opposite direction.

Obviously, I'd hurt his feelings.

"Aw, Rex," I started to say. "I'm really, really sorry. . . ."

Just then, I heard a *click-clack* behind us. I jumped up on all four paws.

"Sunny? Are you in here?"

Annie! My princess was here at last!

Annie appeared from around a corner, fanning herself with a pink paper fan. James was right behind her, fanning his face with his hand. He was poking fun at his sister! James always does that.

More than anything, I wanted to leap into Annie's arms and show her how much I loved her. But I was just too worn-out from the heat.

Come over to me, Annie, I thought.

"Aw, Sunny," Annie said, as if she could read my mind. She crouched down and tickled my left ear. "Well, you found your own air conditioner, didn't you? You lucky dog! It's nice and cool down here on the tiled floor, isn't it?"

I looked up at her and panted a little. I was the luckiest dog, wasn't I?

Rex didn't wait for James to come over to him. He greeted his prince with a howl. He bounced up and dashed between James's legs. That dog looked like he was playing a game of Catch Me If You Can!

"ARRROOOWWWOOO!"

"Hey," James giggled. "Chill out, Rex!"

"Chill out? How can he when it feels like a hundred degrees in here?" Annie joked.

"Very funny, sis," James said.

James finally caught Rex after a little chase in the hall. The prince squeezed the beagle in his arms. Rex turned and planted a big, wet lick onto James's face.

"Yuck!" James moaned, wiping off the drool with the back of his hand. "Whatcha do that for, dude?"

Rex did it again!

"Blecch, DOG!"

James was so grossed out that he let go! Rex wriggled right out of James's arms and landed on all fours. Then, glancing around as if waiting to make sure the coast was clear, Rex took off like he'd been fired out of a cannon.

"Rex!" James bellowed.

Rex didn't stop to listen. He scooted left and right and around the sofa and the curio cabinets. And he knew exactly what he was doing! Rex had this knowing smirk on his puppy face. Like the smirk he'd worn the time he smashed a palace vase to bits or the time he cracked a glass door by sliding into it sideways. Rex thinks acting crazy is just fun.

Annie, James, and I tried to get Rex to slow down. Chasing after him, we slipped. We slid. We nearly fell down ourselves!

"Come back," Annie cried.

"Listen to me!" James yelled.

"S-T-O-O-O-O-O-OP!" a third human voice called out from the hallway. All of us froze in our tracks—including Rex.

We turned to see who had yelled.

In the doorway, Nanny Sarah stood there with her beautiful red hair twisted into a bun on top of her head. She was wearing a flowered sundress and sandals. In her arms was a pile of plush towels.

I glanced over at Annie and James.

They looked nervous, but they were still smiling.

At the palace, Nanny Sarah cared for the

princess and prince, while we dogs were looked after by Nanny Fran. But some days, Nanny Sarah was in charge of us, too.

"Well!" Nanny Sarah said, clearing her throat. "What's going on in here? Trouble?"

"W—w—we're . . ." Annie stammered in a soft voice. "Sorry, Nanny Sarah. We were just . . ."

"Aren't you hot enough without all this running around?" Nanny Sarah exclaimed. "There's a heat wave in the kingdom. If you aren't careful, you might melt!"

James shrugged and smiled. "Yeah," he said, wiping his forehead, which was dripping with sweat. "I'm already melting."

Rex and I jumped, and we panted very loudly. That made Nanny Sarah a little testy.

"Settle down!" Nanny Sarah told us. "I have a surprise for all of you, dogs included. But we need to settle down before we do anything else. . . ."

"Did you say a surprise?" Annie squealed.

James's eyes lit up and he rushed over to Nanny Sarah's side. "What is it? What is it?"

My tail began to wag uncontrollably.

I love a *surprise*.

Rex's tail wagged, too. In fact, our tails were thumping so hard that our bodies moved from side to side like windup toys.

*Tell us about the surprise! Tell us! TELL US!*

"Tell us, Nanny Sarah!" Annie cried.

"Please!" James begged.

Nanny Sarah laughed as she put the fluffy towels down on a table.

"Well, my dears, since it is so hot today," she said, "King Jon and Queen Katherine have given us permission to do something we have not done in a long time. And I have been working on our plan all morning!"

My mind raced with questions. *What plan was she talking about? What were we doing? Where were we going? Was there ice cream involved?*

The best things in life always involved ice cream.

Rex raced over to Nanny Sarah and began twisting in the air like a circus dog. James tried to get him to stop, but Rex was being Rex. He kept right on jumping.

Nanny Sarah leaned down and looked Rex square in the eye.

"If you aren't a good palace puppy, Rex, we

won't be able to go anywhere," she warned him.

Rex sat still and looked up at Nanny Sarah.

She glanced at us and at the prince and princess. "You must *all* be on your very best behavior, understood? Children *and* dogs."

We sat there in silence for a moment, trying to be good. But it was no use. James finally blurted out, "Please tell us! What's the surprise?"

"Where are we going?" Annie asked. "Tell us!"

Nanny Sarah made her announcement at last: "Glimmer Rock Beach!" she cried.

"The beach?" Annie and James screamed in unison. "Wahoo!"

Now *they* were the ones jumping in the air like crazy circus pups.

# Chapter 2

Rex chased my tail. Whenever we got truly overexcited, Rex and I would climb all over each other, almost like we were dancing. We started doing this after we saw James and Annie dance at a palace ball. I thought that if people could dance, why couldn't puppies?

Unfortunately, we usually twirled too fast.

That means we crash-landed too hard.

Today, we fell to the floor in a heap and howled with glee. Nanny Sarah didn't look mad this time.

"Oh, Rex and Sunny, I'm happy to be getting out of this hot palace, too," she said with a smile. "At the beach, we'll play in the surf and cool off, and it will be a fantastic afternoon. . . ."

15

"You just need to behave," Annie added.

"I'm going to swim in the ocean, and you can't stop me!" Rex yelled, dancing around me.

"How, Rex? You've never even been to the beach," I told him. "You don't even know how to swim!"

"Fiddlesticks! I'm going to swim with the sharks!" Rex cried.

I sighed to myself.

*Oh, dear.*

This was going to be an interesting trip, for sure. In my head, I could almost hear a seagull squawking and smell the salty beach air that was waiting for us.

Rex stuck his snout into the air.

*"Rowwaarrrrf!"* he barked happily, even though he probably didn't know exactly what he was happy about.

That beagle really thought that he would be swimming with sharks! But there were no sharks at Glimmer Rock Beach!

James scooped Rex up in one arm. "We have to get ready!"

They headed upstairs.

Annie seized me and lifted me high into the

air. "You need to be good today, Sunny!" she said, holding me out in front of her nose as we followed James and Rex upstairs. "I don't want you and Rex getting into mischief now or later, okay? Nanny Sarah is in charge today, and she means business. One false move and our beach day will be ruined. Got it?"

I nodded my golden head and whimpered. *Got it.*

Upstairs in the bedroom, things felt a little bit cooler than they had downstairs. A fan whirred in one corner, and the curtains blew in the breeze. Annie dropped me on top of her bed and started searching through her dresser drawers.

"I have to find my purple bathing suit and my terry cloth shorts. This is going to be so much fun!"

"Hey!" James poked his head into her room. He had a pair of swim trunks on, and carried a snorkel mask in his hand. Rex scampered through the door. "Is Nanny Sarah making lunch?" James asked.

"Chef Dilly is making lunch," Annie replied. "I think he's making peanut-butter-and-banana sandwiches."

Rex made his *YUM!* face and licked his lips. I was thinking the same thing: Give me food!

"Drat!" James snapped his fingers. "We should get lunch *at* the beach. I love those ice-cream cones from the Snack Shack."

"Ice cream isn't lunch," Annie said. "It isn't a sandwich!"

"Sure it is," James said. "Haven't you ever heard of an *ice-cream* sandwich?"

I had to admit that my stomach growled when I heard the words *ice cream*. Some human words sounded better than others, and the words *ice cream* were definitely two of them. Even better than peanut butter and bananas!

I was feeling hungry all of a sudden.

"Did someone mention the Snack Shack?" Nanny Sarah asked, appearing at Annie's door. In her hands she carried some oversized tote bags with the McDougal crest embroidered across one side. "It's not a beach day without ice cream to cool us down! Of course we'll go there!"

Annie and James smiled and threw their hands up for a high five. I gave Rex a high five with my paw!

"Here are the bags to pack your things," Nanny

Sarah said, handing McDougal totes to both James and Annie. "We have towels and blankets. But there are plenty of other things we need to bring. The maid is getting the umbrellas and the larger items."

"Hey, Annie, you pack the swimming stuff and sunscreen. I'll go downstairs and get the boogie boards and stuff," James said. "Come on, Rex! Follow me!"

James and Rex darted out of the room, nearly knocking Nanny Sarah off her feet as they left.

"ROWF!" I barked. I romped over to Nanny Sarah as if to say, *Are you okay?*

Nanny Sarah scratched the top of my head and made a kissy-face. Sometimes she talks to me like I'm a little baby, but I don't mind one bit. I love getting her attention.

"I will tell the palace chauffeur to be ready in fifteen minutes, okay, girls?" she told me and the princess. "Now, shake a leg!"

As Nanny Sarah left the room, I actually shook my back leg, trying to be cute.

Annie saw me and grinned. "Don't worry about Rex getting into trouble," she whispered, reaching down to stroke my floppy ear. "Remember the time he ran through a puddle of paint and tracked paw prints all over one of the antique royal carpets?"

I nodded. I also remembered the time, during a birthday party for our cousin Jackson, that Rex raced in to attack the many-layered birthday cake.

I remembered *lots* of Rex-tastrophes.

"He's a good puppy," Annie said, grinning. "He just—gets a little too excited sometimes. But he will be good at the beach."

Turning back to her closet, Annie reached for some clothes and books and shoved them into the tote bag. I stretched out on the plush carpet next to my doggy bed, crossed my paws, and just watched. She packed like we were going on a week's vacation! Did we really need so many things? We were just going down the road to Glimmer Rock Beach. How many books could one girl read? Wasn't she planning to spend time at the beach playing with me? Why was she packing *two* sundresses?

Annie threw more things into her bag: sparkly flip-flops; a straw hat with a yellow ribbon tied above the brim; and a bottle of coconut sunblock.

I loved how it smelled when she rubbed it on her arms. Mmmmm . . . coconut! Then again, I loved *all* smells.

I wished Annie could read my mind and knew to pack all the things I wanted to bring today, too:

- An entire package of glazed Beefy Biscuits
- A doggy towel with embroidered paw prints and my name, Sunny, printed on the side in big red letters
- My favorite yellow Frisbee (the worn one with chew marks)
- My rhinestone collar that sparkles like Glimmer Rock
- My water dish (That newspaper said to drink lots of water!)

When she finished packing, Annie asked me to jump on top of the bag so she could squish and zip it. When I got on top, Annie was able to yank the zipper closed.

"Thanks, Sunny," Annie said. "You are as good as gold."

I beamed.

Of course I was as good as gold. I was a goldendoodle!

"Rex!"

I heard the shout from downstairs. Annie and I rushed out the door and sped down the wide staircase. The carpets had all been vacuumed. The banisters shone with polish.

Apparently, the polish was the source of the problem.

Standing at the bottom of the stairs was Nanny Sarah, arms crossed tightly in front of her chest. At her feet was Rex, drenched in soapy water.

A puddle stretched from him to an empty

bucket across the hall. A palace servant stood there, hanging his head, an enormous sponge in his hand. He'd been the one cleaning the staircase.

"Look at the mess you made!" James cried at Rex.

Nanny Sarah held up one hand to speak. Even from the top of the stairs I could feel her stern stare.

"Rex McDougal," she began. "I don't know what to do with you. . . ."

Rex cowered at James's feet.

"Please don't be mad," James tried to explain. "He didn't mean to do it, Nanny Sarah—"

"Well!" Nanny Sarah said. "This kind of

behavior will not do in the palace. And puppies who misbehave do *not* deserve to go to the beach."

Everyone got really quiet, even Rex. I saw him pull his tail tightly under his legs. His fur was sopping wet. Annie and I went downstairs.

"Perhaps we *shouldn't* bring the pets on our little beach trip," Nanny Sarah said.

I felt my puppy jaw clench. What? No! Was this really happening? *Say something, Annie! Say something, James!* Why weren't they saying anything? Nanny Sarah wouldn't leave us here at the sweltering palace all day, would she? She wouldn't promise us a day at the beach and then take it away, would she?

"Please!" Annie cried at last. "Nanny Sarah, we can't go without the puppies. We *have* to bring the puppies."

"Oh?" Nanny Sarah said. "Why is that?"

"Rex has never been to the beach!" James said.

Nanny Sarah's eyebrows went up. "And?"

"He's never really been anywhere except the palace."

"So?" Nanny Sarah said, making a stern face.

"*Ruff!*" I barked to get Rex's attention.

"*Ruff! Ruff!* Do you hear her? We need to be good puppies," I said, "or else we can't go to the beach!"

Before I could say another word, he rolled over onto his back and stuck his paws in the air, like he was playing dead.

"Oh!" Nanny Sara cracked a smile.

"Awww!" Annie laughed, pointing at Rex's speckled belly. "He's just kidding around."

James leaned in for a tickle. Rex squealed with delight. He tried everything he could to show Nanny Sarah that he was just a silly, happy puppy who wanted to go to the beach. Was it working?

"James, you must promise me that Rex will be good," Nanny Sarah insisted.

"He will love swimming and making sand castles as much as Sunny does," James said. "Right, Annie? I promise."

"We *both* promise!" Annie said.

"Well," Nanny Sarah said, raising one eyebrow, "if you and Annie both promise that the dogs will be good, then I won't keep them home in all this heat." She clapped her hands. "Now . . . let's shake a—"

"Leg!" Annie cried. She, James, Rex, and I all shook our legs at the exact same time.

"Aren't you the clever crew!" Nanny Sarah said, smirking.

"Let's go," James said. "That ocean is calling to me. I'll get the beach tent."

"Don't forget to grab the superstrong leash for Rex, too!" Annie called after him. "Just in case . . ."

"Rrrrrrrrroooof!" Rex woofed.

Quickly, Annie and I dashed back upstairs to get her tote bag. I found my Frisbee in a corner of the room.

We met James and Rex back in the hall, and Nanny Sarah gave instructions to Edward, the chauffeur.

Edward dragged Annie's and James's bags from the stairs to the limousine. I could see from the look on Nanny Sarah's face as he passed by that she thought we'd packed way too much.

But Edward was able to stuff everything into the trunk, including a bag containing mermaid-shaped toys, plastic cars, and neon-yellow shovels.

James lugged the boogie boards from a downstairs closet. Edward heaved those into the limousine trunk, too, along with a beach umbrella and our giant red cooler. I loved the color red so much—and not just because it perfectly complemented my golden coat. Annie had said once that the color red meant a lot of things, like power and courage. And I am one courageous palace puppy!

Right now, I was hoping the color red meant *great time at the beach*.

"Sunny," Annie said in a sweet voice, "I remembered something extra for you. . . ." She reached into the pocket of her sundress and pulled out a Snappy Snap. "Eat up! You deserve it."

I perked right up when I saw the bone-shaped biscuit with its white sugar glaze. My favorite! I crunched down hard and chewed the cookie to bits. She tossed one to Rex, too, of course. My Annie never left any puppy out. Then she clipped on my purple waterproof collar (which I admit was way more practical than the rhinestone one) and we were ready to go!

I began to imagine all the *good* things that would happen at the beach. Was it possible for the five of us—Rex included—to have a quiet, peaceful, and trouble-free time?

"*RRRRROOOOOOOWWWWOOOOO!*" Rex

howled. He turned to me. "Let's go make some waves!" he barked.

I shot him a look. "What kind of waves?" I asked, worried that he was already planning trouble.

"The wet, salty kind!" Rex barked back.

And we followed Nanny Sarah, James, and Annie out to the car with our tails wagging.

# Chapter 3

We bid a friendly farewell to the palace guard standing by the front door. He wore a uniform with epaulets and brass buttons.

I wondered whether there was a uniform like that for dogs. I would have looked very good in an outfit with golden buttons to match my fur coat.

The guard waved as we paraded down the flight of stone steps and hopped into our limousine.

Whoa! The car's air conditioner hit like an arctic blast! Now, *that* was cool.

Rex, James, and Nanny Sarah sat across from me and Annie.

"To the beach, Edward!" Nanny Sarah called

out, tapping the glass partition between the front and back of the limousine. "Glimmer Rock Beach!"

Annie lifted me up so I could see out the window. I put my front paws on the door and pressed my nose to the glass.

It felt *cold*! My puppy temperature went way down.

Our palace was set back from the main roads. It was surrounded by woods, meadows, and other estates. Edward slowly drove all the way down our rambling, tree-lined driveway. Then the limo turned on to a local road. We drove past a wide field planted with bushes, trees, and flowers of all kinds and colors. Soon enough, we were on the turnpike, heading east for the coast.

A vent near the rear door chilled the tips of my ears. But I kept my nose pressed right up to the window so I could see everything.

After a long drive, I spotted the sign I'd been looking for all this time: EXIT 7A, GLIMMER ROCK BEACH.

Being able to read came in handy at times like this!

I glanced over at Rex. He was sniffing his tail,

so of course he didn't even notice the sign. That figured!

My puppy pulse quickened. One more exit and we would be there! I imagined sand between my paws.

Edward exited at 7A, and the limousine twisted its way through the main streets of Glimmer Rock.

There were so many things out there that we never got to see at the palace:

People roller-skating.

Boats attached to the backs of cars.

Bicycles built for two.

Other dogs walking—leash-free!

In my imagination, I saw myself running along the sidewalk next to Annie, my fur flying, my paws romping on the grassy parts.

Of course, Nanny Sarah usually did not allow me to run free without a leash. But a royal dog could dream, couldn't she?

There were many requirements for royal dogs. We had to spend most of our time doing royal things and acting proper.

Rex didn't always understand that, but I did.

Royal puppies had to sit pretty at important tea parties and listen when the king and queen issued orders. We had to dine in the large ballroom, eating out of silver dishes. We had to remember who we were, no matter what: royalty. Even when we'd rather have been chasing butterflies or fetching sticks!

That rule went double at the beach.

"Rowf!" I barked softly, to get Rex's attention in the limo.

His tail wagged. "What?" he asked.

"Don't forget to listen to Nanny Sarah when we get to the beach," I said. "No running off."

"I know, I know," Rex said. He pushed me out of the way and pressed his nose right up against the car window.

Rex's wagging tail nearly socked me in the head. I protested, but Annie grabbed me tight.

"Hey!" She planted a kiss on my head. "We're here, Sunny! Isn't this fun?"

The limousine drove through an iron gate with a green sign that read DUNE ROAD. My little heart beat hard inside my chest. I took in a deep breath of air-conditioning and braced myself for the hot sun.

We pulled in to a sandy lot with parked cars. Nanny Sarah stepped out of the limousine. She opened the rear car door wide so we could all get out at the same time.

As we emerged, Annie clipped on my leash. The heat almost knocked me flat. It was actually

hotter here than it had been at the palace. The newspaper had said it would be nearly a hundred degrees. It felt more like *two* hundred!

James tried to put on Rex's leash. Of course, Rex pushed and squirmed his way out the door before the leash went on. James hadn't been holding on very tightly.

"Rex!" James cried, scrambling after his puppy.

Where was Rex running in this heat? I could barely move.

"Everyone, stay together!" Nanny Sarah commanded. "We don't want any trouble!"

No trouble? Ha! Rex's middle name was Trouble.

Luckily, James caught Rex in the nick of time. He grabbed his tail and Rex yelped, but he stopped. James nearly lost his footing. His sunglasses flew off the tip of his nose. I retrieved them from where they'd landed, in the sand.

"You can't run away," I warned Rex again. "Nanny will send us home. She means it."

"Fine," Rex said.

But he was sniffing at the air. I knew he had *another* getaway plan.

Nanny Sarah told us to wait on the other side

of the parking lot while she and Edward unpacked the limousine.

Annie and James held the leashes while we stood next to an enormous wooden sign and waited.

Since I am a much better reader than Rex, I read the sign aloud to him:

## Glimmer Rock Beach Rules

- No Swimming When Red Flag Is Flying
- No Surfing
- No Fishing
- No Glass Bottles
- No Throwing Objects
- No Bicycles or Skateboards on Boardwalk
- No Small Children Left Unattended in Surf
- Pets Allowed Only with Lifeguard on Duty

THANK YOU FOR FOLLOWING THE RULES!

"Rules are for people, not puppies," Rex growled at me.

"No, rules are for *everyone*," I said. "Even royal puppies. Even you."

Rex sniffed in the opposite direction. He started moving away from the sign. He was so good at getting distracted!

"Rex," I whispered. "You promised you would be good today. These are rules we have to follow. . . ."

"Puppies are supposed to have fun," Rex protested, tugging at his leash. "How can I have fun with so many rules?"

Rex had fooled me more than once with logic like that. Last winter, he had actually convinced me to try out sledding in the palace backyard, only not on a sled. He found this pile of fancy-shmancy place mats in the palace kitchen. We ruined the place mats and got into trouble, of course.

Rex tugged at his leash again. He was chewing on it, too.

"Stay still," James said.

But staying still was the last thing Rex wanted to do.

"I smell fish!" Rex yelped at me. He kept

tugging. "Sunny, come on! What are you waiting for? I don't want to stay still."

"No, we have to wait," I said. "Nanny Sarah told us to wait."

Across the lot, I watched Edward and Nanny Sarah take the boogie boards and the last of the bags out of the car. But Rex wasn't watching them. He had his eye on a seagull. Rex was ready to fly away with that bird!

"You think Edward will be swimming with us today?" Annie asked.

"Why? He's not a lifeguard, silly," James said. "Besides, he can't get his transmitters wet or sandy."

Edward had these cool walkie-talkies. I'd seen him use them inside the limousine. He's officially the chauffeur, but he sometimes serves as palace security, too. Someone was always needed to follow the king and queen whenever the royal family went out in public. Security was even more important when the princess and prince were outside the palace gates.

Our monogrammed bags, cooler, and the other stuff from the car was placed on top of a special trolley that had been stored in the limousine. Nanny Sarah and Edward were strong. They pulled it onto the sandy and crowded boardwalk without a problem.

Along the sides of the path were large bushes and overgrown vines. When a bunch of birds flew out with a clatter, I jumped off to the side.

Rex laughed at my reaction.

I liked surprises, but not that kind of surprise!

A few kids zoomed between and past us, shooting water pistols and laughing. They were all wet and covered with sand. One of them squirted and sprayed me! At first I was afraid, but when I barked, they ran off.

Nanny Sarah turned around to check on us when she heard me barking.

Annie told me to carry one of the small boogie boards in my mouth. I think she just wanted to keep me quiet. But it was a good job for me. Goldendoodles have soft mouths. We can nuzzle and bite and it doesn't hurt a bit.

As we walked along, I felt a little dizzy. The intense heat made everything fuzzy! I wanted a water bowl or some kind of snack. Mostly, I wanted to sit. It would have been nice to finally stretch out on my special beach towel and just cool it for a little while.

Rex had totally different plans. As the deep blue-green ocean came partly into view, he got extra-excited. He twisted and turned, wrapping the leash around him every which way. "Big waves, here I come!" he cried.

James was having a hard time hanging on to the leash with all that twisting, and then . . .

*SNAP!*

The leash was worn a little in one spot, so when Rex finally pulled too hard, it snapped easily in two.

James went flying.

"Oh, no!" Nanny Sarah cried. "Quick, somebody, catch that beagle before he gets away again!"

# Chapter 4

Everything happened very fast after that.

Rex (still wearing his ripped leash) darted off the path and toward a stretch of tall sea grass. James got his balance again. He chased Rex, trying to tackle him. But tackling a moving beagle isn't easy.

I pulled hard on my own leash and practically dragged Annie into the sea grass. In the process, I stepped on something sharp. *YOUCH!* Annie bent over and plucked the object out of my paw. I think it was a piece of clamshell.

"Calm down," she whispered, stroking my head.

But I couldn't stay calm! Rex had run off! I needed to go after him.

Annie decided to go with me. We chased Rex from the tall weeds back onto the boardwalk, past Nanny Sarah and Edward and all the piled-up stuff from the car. The other people stepped aside as we all raced past. We nearly collided with half of them!

"Hey!" I barked, with the boogie board still in my mouth, hoping Rex could hear me. "Where are you going, Rex? We'll both get in trouble for this!"

"R-E-E-E-E-E-E-E-E-E-E-E-EX!" James was ahead of me, screeching loudly.

Then, without warning, Rex turned around and charged back toward me. Just like that! And then he stopped. He stopped dead in his tracks!

Maybe he understood that there were rules and he needed to follow them? Maybe royal Rex had had a change of heart?

"Aha!" James ran toward the puppy, rubbing his hands together. "Gotcha, Rex!"

Of course, the prince hadn't really gotten Rex. What he'd gotten was *lucky*. Because sitting smack-dab in the middle of the path was an enormous rottweiler. Rex and half a leash were no match for that massive dog. So he'd stopped short.

"*Rowf?*" Rex tilted his head to one side. He'd

never seen such a big dog! His face said, *Curses, foiled again.* I knew he wanted to race far, far away.

James scooped Rex into his arms.

So far, this whole day had been rather funny—not what I'd expected. Our trip to the beach had been a game of chase.

I couldn't help laughing at all the misadventures so far. What else could possibly happen at the beach?

Something told me *plenty*!

Most people don't think puppies actually laugh, but we do. It's a combination of snorting and panting. We laugh hysterically at bugs buzzing around our heads. We laugh at bubbles. And we always laugh at things that look just plain ridiculous.

Like Rex's face at that exact moment.

I was giggling at James, too, and at his loud neon-orange board shorts and at his sunglasses, which were as big as his head.

*What a bunch of royals we were!*

"RRRRRUFF!" Rex barked.

"Rex, you are a naughty puppy!" Nanny Sarah said, wagging her finger at both of us puppies as she came over. "I told you at the palace that I needed everyone to stick together." She looked at Annie and James. "You two need to control your puppies at the beach, or we will have to head back to the palace," she said sternly. "Give me the beagle."

Rex whimpered as James passed him to Nanny Sarah.

The prince and princess were embarrassed; I could tell. I barked to let them both know that I had been a good puppy. But they were still a little upset at Nanny Sarah's scolding.

Thankfully, while all this chasing around was going on, Edward had found us an excellent spot to set up camp for the afternoon. It was a perfectly smooth stretch of sand with a little shade. He put up the big red umbrella and the beach tent in the middle of everything, with towels and chairs spread out all around. I carried the boogie board right over!

Nanny Sarah led the way to the beach chairs and told us to settle down. She stuck Rex inside the beach tent.

I heard him whimpering and poked my head inside. "What's going on?" I asked.

Annie and James came into the tent a moment after that.

"Excuse me, but we need to get ready to swim!" Annie declared, pushing James out of the tent so she'd have a little privacy for changing.

"ROWF!" I barked, happy to be with my princess again.

"You know what?" Rex said. "You worry too much."

"I worry?" I cried, laughing. Then I grinned. Rex was right. I *did* worry. A lot. I would have to stop doing it—and start having fun.

Annie changed, and we exited the tent. What a view! There were so many people sunbathing. Their skin glowed brown. As the sunlight caught the tips of waves, it made the water look white. The reflection of sun off Glimmer Rock Beach itself seemed to shine a spotlight on us. That sand was so hot!

"Come along, children!" Nanny Sarah called out. "I want to put some sunblock on your arms and faces before you get burned. . . ."

Annie grinned at me. She had on a cute purple one-piece swimsuit and a floppy hat, and she was ready to swim!

James put on a T-shirt that read, "I ♥ Dogs."

Rex looked up at James, wagging his tail. He knew what that T-shirt said.

Nanny Sarah applied the lotion.

James leaned down to Rex. "I know you want to walk around, but you need to stay close by," he said. "One more stunt like you pulled earlier and we'll never be able to come back to the beach. So, please, be a good dog? I'll leave you here with the superstrong leash. Good thing we brought it!"

James hooked Rex's new leash to one of the tent stakes so he wouldn't wander off.

"Hey, Rex, why do you always get into trouble?" I asked.

"You say *trouble* like it's a bad thing," Rex said, smirking, with a glint in his eye. I could tell he was already pulling at the leash a little bit, trying to undo it. Was he hatching another escape plan? "I don't know why I have to keep this on," he whined.

"Well," I mumbled, "you did run away. *Twice.*"

"Where am I going to go now?" Rex asked.

I laughed. "Are you serious?" I glanced around the beach. "Anywhere!"

I flung myself down onto a plush beach towel at a good distance from Rex. If he was going to get into trouble again, I'd stay as far away as possible.

As I let the ocean breeze ruffle my fur, I took in the view. There was a large sand dune that stretched and rose behind my head like a skyscraper. I overheard Nanny Sarah tell James and Annie that the dune had been created by something called erosion. That was when the ocean came in and washed away some of the beach. Over a long period of time, it left behind a large, sandy cliff.

Under the towering dune, I felt like the teeniest dog in the whole world. The blue sky seemed bluer than I'd ever seen it before. The sea air felt good on my whiskers.

I wanted to take off running down the beach and feel the wind blowing through my fur! I wanted to dance in the surf and get my paws soaking wet!

It was so beautiful that I almost forgot about Rex.

Almost.

*Be patient, Sunny,* I told myself. *Soon, Nanny Sarah will take us all down to the water's edge, and we can jump in together! Rex will stop causing trouble! Soon!*

I hoped my patience would hold out in all this heat.

Nanny Sarah tilted the umbrella a little bit in the sand so its shadow would block the sun. She threw down two more of the large blankets she had brought so Rex could lie down.

"Okay, Rex," she said. "I'm going to take off your leash now, but you had better be good."

Nanny Sarah unclipped Rex's collar and let him go free. I waited for him to run. But he didn't. Rex sniffed a towel and rubbed up against Nanny Sarah's leg as if to say, *Thanks.*

Annie opened the red cooler and filled the doggy bowls. I ran back, and Rex and I both lapped up the cool water right away. Wow! This heat was unbearable. If it hadn't been for the tent and the umbrellas, we'd have had no relief. But the beach was still way better than the palace, thanks to that sea breeze.

After drinking some water, Rex got his energy

back and he still didn't run! I was impressed. He began digging a hole in the sand nearby.

Now, this would have been a fine activity, except for one thing: Rex kept kicking all the sand back onto *our* blankets! And when James told him to stop, he didn't; he just switched locations and kicked sand onto someone *else's* blankets! What a mess!

Edward and James began to shout. Nanny Sarah looked miserable. I feared the worst again. Was she getting ready to pack everything up and get out of there?

Thankfully, Rex stopped kicking sand. He got distracted again. He had found a crab in the sand.

A boy in yellow shorts snapped a picture of Rex and the crab. The boy seemed to know we were from the palace.

Other people, too, recognized us and the princess and prince. They stared.

A girl and her friend started whispering. Were they talking about me and Princess Annie?

The guy in the black suit with the walkie-talkie who helped to set up our beach tent and umbrella was a dead giveaway. We were not your ordinary beachcombers.

Now, I like a good photo op as much as the next royal pooch, but after a few minutes, a crowd began to gather. A girl in a polka-dot bikini snapped a photo with a camera phone. Some boys also took pictures of us. One of the boys said something about having an album of dog photographs. With all the cameras clicking, it felt like the paparazzi were there. We'd been discovered!

This was one of the perks—and disadvantages—of being royalty. Once people found out who we were, they often treated us differently. I never fully understood that, although I knew it bugged Annie. I'd heard her talk about it sometimes.

Annie and James, as the princess and prince, were homeschooled by a tutor at the palace. Sometimes it was hard for them to see all the kids their age in Glimmer Rock and not be able just to hang out with them. That was true for the royal pups, too!

We all tried to ignore the photographers and the kids nearby, but it was tough. Tough for everyone, that is, except Rex. By now he'd posed for many photos for passersby, with and without his crab friend. He jumped around, biting at the air like a real show-off. Rex was getting overexcited again. Thankfully, he stayed near the tent.

I tried to focus on the squawks of the seagulls and the steady swoosh of waves lapping the shore. My eyes closed. I felt cooler as I inhaled the sweet sea air.

Before too long, I drifted into a deep, beach sleep. And as I dozed off, I started to dream.

In my dream, I made myself a famous movie star. The cameras around me were paparazzi. Everybody wanted my *paw*tograph.

Then Nanny Sarah gave me a giant dish of Beefy Deluxe dog food with bacon bits and a delicious, cold ice pop.

*"Ruff! Ruff!"* I barked in delight.

There is nothing like a doggy dream to make everything seem right with the world.

# Chapter 5

"Leave it alone!"

I heard Annie shout, and I jumped up onto my paws. *Whoa.* I nearly lost my balance. My head was spinning. I was hot and groggy.

What was going on? Where was I?

It sure was tough to stand up quickly when I'd been knocked out just a moment earlier. Had I been asleep a long time?

"I want the blue one!" James cried.

"No, I want it!" Annie said. "I called it first."

"No, I did."

"*I* did!" James squealed.

I blinked hard and looked across at my princess and her brother. They were each holding on to one end of a boogie board. I knew we'd packed two boards—pink for Annie and blue for James—but now they both wanted to use the blue one?

Annie said that apparently the blue one rode the waves better, because that color blended in with the water.

Annie and James continued to bicker. They got louder and louder, too, to the point where I jumped up and went over to them with a loud *ruff* of my own.

"Hey!" shouted James.

"Watch it!" Annie said. I think she was talking to James, but she could have been talking to me.

"RAAAAARF!" I barked, standing between them. But no one listened.

I grabbed the boogie board in my mouth. *That* would get their attention and get them to stop their fuss.

"Let go of that!" Annie cried as soon as I'd grabbed it in my soft mouth. "Sunny, stop!"

"Yeah, stop!" James added.

Normally, I would have listened and obeyed. I always did. But for some reason, this time I didn't let go. The three of us held on to that board, tugging back and forth, back and forth. Five minutes must have passed. I was proud of myself, too, hanging on like that without biting into it with my teeth. Of course, I'd had practice earlier, carrying it to the beach.

And then, without warning, the princess and prince dropped the board at exactly the same time, and it came crashing back onto my head!

Annie and James froze. "Sunny!" they cried at the same time.

I wasn't really hurt, but I was dizzy.

My princess reached down and rubbed my head. Her hands were soothing.

I whined. Then I looked up at James with my widest puppy-dog eyes.

"Hey, Sunny, I'm sorry the board slammed into you," James said. "But why did you grab it?"

"No, the question is why did *you* grab it, James?" Annie asked. "I told you I wanted the blue one. But you insisted on hanging on. . . ."

"You wanted the blue one? And I'm supposed to take the pink one?" James asked. "You're crazy, sis. *Craaaaaazy.*"

"ROWWWWROOOO!" I howled. I hated it when James called Annie names like that. Why couldn't they just stop arguing?

"You kids okay?" Edward said, coming over. "Nanny Sarah will be right back with the ice pops. I can see her from here," he added, looking through his binoculars. "You'd better behave."

*Mmmmmm. Ice pops? Just like in my dream?*

I sniffed my way from our chairs and towels, from the boogie boards, and back up to the boardwalk we had followed onto the beach. I don't know exactly what I was sniffing for, but there were so many great smells. I got a little excited.

When the tide came in, it went all the way up to the edge of the beach. There was a lot of junk on this beach's tidal line: paper, plastic, and an old buoy tied with rope. Even the best beaches get stuff washed ashore. And there was beach tar, too! I was careful not to step into it. Tar takes forever to wash off paws.

Before I knew it, I'd gone a fair distance from the chairs and towels. Everyone was far, far away!

My princess Annie saw me and waved. I wagged my tail so she'd know I could see her. I raced back for ice pops. Nanny Sarah was back!

As I trotted over to them, I looked around for Rex. He hadn't gotten into the whole argument between James and Annie. Normally, that was exactly the kind of action Rex would have found exciting. He had a snout for trouble—and for troublesome talk.

"Ice pops for everyone!" Nanny Sarah declared. There were so many flavors to choose from— lemon, berry, watermelon—and I wanted to try all of them! Everyone, including Edward and Nanny Sarah, sat down on the towels and began to taste all the flavors. There was nothing like the taste of something sweet and icy on a triple-digit-temperature day like today.

I lay down with my pop between my paws and licked. "Rex?" I barked. I scanned the chairs and towels. Where had that pooch gone?

With the pop melting in my mouth, I hopped up and walked around the big red umbrella. Rex wasn't in the tent, either.

I sensed that beagle—somewhere. But where?

I got a weird feeling in the pit of my puppy tummy. Something was wrong. As much as that dog and I fight and tease, it's hard to imagine doing almost anything without him around. Rex is my brother and my best friend. It was weird to think that he was . . . well, missing.

"Ruff! Ruff! Brrrrrrowf!" I called out, hoping that he was close by, hiding or playing.

But there was no Rex anywhere. Did Nanny Sarah and the others notice? How was it possible—especially after everything that had already happened today—*not* to realize that Rex was gone?

"WAWWAROOO!" I barked, looking high and low. I checked behind the red cooler. I checked under every blanket and towel.

I knew Rex had been wild all morning. He'd run away before. But what if Rex had gotten into real trouble here on the beach? What if he had been dognapped?

This was a big—no, a *huge*—beach. I needed to find him now, before he got into serious trouble.

I scanned up and down the beach.

Row after row of people sunbathed next to brightly colored umbrellas. A few birds circled at the shoreline. I made a note to myself: *remember to chase seagulls later*. Finding Rex was more important right now.

"ROWF!" I barked, thinking that maybe, just maybe, Rex might hear.

But barking was useless. Between the water and the people, there was just too much noise around for any dog—or anyone—to hear me.

I poked my nose high up in the air and let out a slow howling noise. A few people seated very close to where I was standing gave me a funny look. "Be quiet, dog!" someone yelled.

But how could I be quiet? I was very worried.

There were so many people here, so much ocean, and Rex had never been to the beach before. All it would take would be one sweeping wave to crash over him and he could be dragged out to sea! Or what if he wasn't paying attention while walking along the beach and he fell—*splat!*—into a giant hole that some sand-castle builder had dug on the beach?

I could feel my heart thumping harder inside my goldendoodle chest.

After a few moments of my searching, Annie, James, and Nanny Sarah began to realize what I was doing.

"Rex!" James said as he realized Rex wasn't around.

"REX!" Annie called out.

Nanny Sarah rolled her eyes. "It figures," she said. Rex had misbehaved all morning. Why were James and Annie surprised?

"Arf! Arffffff!" I yelped, trying to be helpful.

Annie crouched down and kissed my head. "It'll be okay, Sunny," she reassured me. "You're such a good dog. Don't worry."

I barked much louder. "ARF! ARF! ARF!"

"Quit barking!" James cried. He spun around in a circle, looking frantically at each beach chair at least three times. "Oh, no!" he said. "There are so many people here! What if someone has stolen him?"

James feared the worst, just like I did. Rex *was* a royal puppy. What if someone had puppy-napped Rex for a real king's ransom? All those people who had been snapping photos . . . Had one of them been up to no good?

"Don't think that, James," Nanny Sarah said, trying to sound reassuring. "We will find Rex. We've got the best sniffer in all the kingdom right here."

Nanny Sarah looked at me when she said that, and I felt proud.

I *was* the best sniffer. And I was determined to put my nose to work! All I had to do was pick up the right scents.

Edward got on his walkie-talkie. He pulled

out a pair of binoculars and began searching the coastline.

We couldn't see that beagle anywhere we looked. It would have been easy for one little dog to disappear on a beach with at least a thousand people baking in the sun. How had Rex gone so far in such a short time?

I had to do something! Maybe I could smell some kind of clue on the beach? Maybe I could smell where Rex had gone?

I would try my best.

That was all a good dog could do.

Sunny to the rescue!

# Chapter 6

I stuck my snout right up into the air and took a
deep whiff.

*Mmmmmmm.*

At first, the only things I smelled in the beach
air were the fruit-smoothie coconut, papaya,
mango, persimmon, and honeysuckle smells that
were from all the people using tropical suntan
lotions and sunblocks.

But then I smelled the clammy scent of the
sea: ocean foam, fish, sand, seaweed, and the hot
breeze, all mixed together.

My nose went nuts. I worked it up and down
the beach. Since it was after high tide, the sand
was soft, and walking on it was tough. I dodged

swimmers and sand castles along the way.

And then I found a line of paw prints. They could have belonged to any old dog. So I sniffed closer.

I smelled something familiar!

As I glanced around, I caught sight of a couple of other pooches. There was a Labrador retriever diving into the water. I spotted a silver-gray spaniel covered in wet sand. There was a bulldog with a sparkly rhinestone collar and leash.

But these prints didn't belong to any of those dogs.

Nanny Sarah was right behind me. She wanted to form a real search party.

"But Sunny, dear, you need to stick with one of us—just in case."

I shook out my coat and licked Nanny Sarah's hand. That was my way of saying, *okeydoke*. Her hand tasted like sunblock.

All at once I caught the scent of something else on the wind, something I hadn't smelled before, something that reminded me even more of Rex.

*Hot dog? Pretzels?* The smells from the food stalls wafted down toward the beach.

Of course, we had not had lunch yet, so the

wafting odor of grilled hot dogs was a delicious surprise. It was all I could think about the moment I smelled it. I was hungry, even after the ice pops.

Hot dogs were one of Rex's favorite foods, too. I wondered if maybe he'd smelled this same smell. If he had, the situation might have gone something like this:

1.    Rex got a whiff of the dogs (the steaming hot, nonbarking kind).
2.    The hot-dog odor sent that beagle pouncing over towels and legs and a dozen falling-down sand castles.
3.    Rex got lost on the beach.
4.    Rex got distracted by the boardwalk.
5.    Rex got taken away by some stranger???

"R-O-O-O-O-O-F!" I barked loudly.

Nanny Sarah gave me a quizzical look. "*Roooof* yourself!" she cried, smiling. "Do you know where Rex is, Sunny?"

"I know that bark!" Annie cooed. "Sunny, do you know where Rex is?"

How I wished I could just bark the words *hot* and *dog*. That would have blown their minds.

I began to take a few steps in the direction of the food. Then I raced back. I did the same move all over again until they understood that I wanted to head toward the boardwalk.

"You want to show us something?" James asked.

I poked my nose into the air and sniffed.

*Sniff, sniff, sniff, YES!*

Annie sniffed the wind, too, after she saw me doing it.

"Sunny smells something."

*Yes, yes, yes!*

James breathed in deeply. "Hot dogs!" he cried. "I smell them, too."

"Perhaps *Rex* smelled them, too?" Nanny Sarah said, tilting her head and looking right at me.

"Rrrruff! Rrrruff!" I barked excitedly.

"That's it!" Annie cried.

"I knew it!" James said, snapping his fingers.

"Yeah, you're a regular genius," Annie said, smirking.

"I am a genius," James said. Then he added, "We're both supersmart. But we can only figure this out if we all work together." James gave Annie a great big high five. They both laughed.

"Maybe working on this together won't be so bad after all," Annie said.

"That's the spirit!" Nanny Sarah cried.

Annie leaned down and stroked my floppy ears. "Well done, Sunny," she said, patting my warm head. Then she turned to Nanny Sarah. "So now what do we do, Sarah? Should we all go up to the boardwalk and visit the hot-dog stand? What if Rex comes back to the tent and towels? Won't he get even more lost and confused if we're all gone?"

Nanny Sarah crossed her arms over her chest. She looked as if she were thinking.

"If we check out the food stands, we visit the food carts for lunch, too," James cried.

"James! How can you think of food when your puppy is missing?" Annie asked.

"I don't know." James shrugged. "Ask my tummy that question. I just ate two ice pops, but I'm still hungry. . . ."

"You just want a double dog with mustard!" Annie cried.

"Nah," James said. "I want a triple dog!"

"Children!" Nanny Sarah held up a finger. "Shhh! You will *both* go to find Rex, with Sunny. How's that for a plan? We need manpower to find this pup. There are so many places to look! But I'm putting Edward in charge. He will *not* tolerate fighting."

Nanny Sarah told us that kingdom security measures required that we not travel anywhere without a grown-up. So Annie, James, Edward, and I went off to search while Nanny Sarah stayed behind with our stuff. She wanted to be there just in case Rex came back.

"Be very careful," Nanny Sarah told Annie as we got ready to go. "Make sure Edward is with you at all times."

"My eyes will be on you three," Edward said. "No racing ahead."

I had a hunch that my hot-dog theory was foolproof. It would take us to Rex.

Hot dogs were Rex's absolute, all-time favorite food. He could eat fifty of those pigs-in-blankets, or mini-hot-dog appetizers, the palace always served for birthday parties and carnivals. Once I saw him eat three in one bite! Another time he was eating from his royal dog dish and one stuck in his snout. That looked so funny!

No matter what Nanny Sarah or the princess said, I was the *true* leader of this mission, and I wasn't going to worry about racing ahead. My paws were revved and ready to search!

I sniffed wildly as we headed to the boardwalk. What a maze of towels and sandals and boogie boards! On the way, Annie got a bright idea. She told us she wanted to make a detour to the lifeguard station.

"Have you seen our dog?" Annie asked when we got there. She described Rex to the lifeguard with the stripe of sunblock on his nose and the giant whistle around his neck. I was good at spying those details.

Of course, it wasn't the first time a dog—or a person—had gotten lost on the busy beach. The lifeguard didn't have much to tell us. But he said he'd keep his eyes open for Rex.

He explained the Glimmer Rock Beach procedures for dealing with this kind of emergency. We could do our own search first, just as we'd planned. If that came up empty, we could file a search-party form, and then various people working at the beach would get involved. We had lots of work to do!

For a guy in a black suit on a hotter than hot day at the beach, Edward was keeping up pretty

well with the quick pace we had set. We had to stay close together. The boardwalk was packed! I didn't want to lose track of anyone, since I was sniffing with my head low to the ground.

It was no wonder that we couldn't find Rex anywhere at first. There were people crowded in ankle to ankle. There must have been a dozen or more food stands there, too. All the smells kind of blended together. I couldn't read the signs, because they were placed too high up.

All I could see was a bunch of flip-flops and food scraps. So much had fallen onto the planks there— it was a regular buffet of pieces of rolls, greasy and overpowdered funnel cakes, fried-chicken-finger bits, plain old ordinary fries, ketchup packets, and popcorn. Everything!

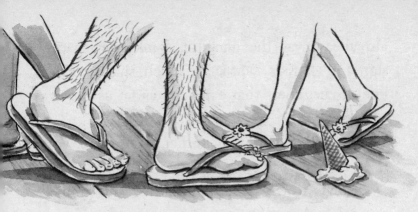

There was a lot of melted gum down there, too. That was extra icky. Between the beach tar and melted gum, I needed to be careful not to get mess on my puppy paws. I stepped very cautiously.

James ran ahead of me and Annie. I thought about racing to catch up with him, but stayed close to Annie. Edward hurried to keep pace with James.

"RRRRRAWF!" I called out, hoping they'd wait for us.

With all the commotion and the many smells, I kept losing my focus. I needed to pick up Rex's scent again, but I kept losing it.

*Focus, Sunny, focus.*

I took a deep doggy breath and started sniffing again. Putting one paw in front of the other, I followed one of the long planks on the boardwalk.

Up ahead was the gigantic, frankfurter-shaped sign for FRANK'S FRANKS, a lunch shack with a line of customers that extended as far as the eye could see.

I sniffed. There was another smell there. Was it . . . the palace? Yes!

"Rowf! Rowf!" I started panting and jumped up against Annie's legs.

"James!" Annie said to her brother. "I think Sunny may have found Rex's scent again! Good dog, Sunny! Good girl!"

I chased my tail around once, happily, and barked again. This was definitely a Rex smell! It was a mixture of dog and air freshener and carpet cleaner, with a hint of bacon. Everything in the palace had smelled stronger that morning because of the heat, and it had all stuck to Rex! Oh, he couldn't be far now. He'd definitely been roaming near Frank's!

Edward muscled into the front of the line. "Let's ask the hot-dog-stand vendor a few questions," he said.

"Excuse me," James asked the vendor, who was wearing a little cap with FRANKS written on top. "Have you seen a dog come around here?"

Frank pulled one of the steaming hot dogs out of the vat in his cart. "You mean a little dog like this one?" he cracked, indicating me.

James and Annie giggled.

"ROWF!" I barked grumpily. This was no time for jokes. Our dog was on the loose!

Was it possible that I missed Rex so much already? Even after he'd annoyed me so much all morning?

The heat made the search harder.

"Frank," Annie continued, addressing the hot-dog guy, "we seem to have lost one of our pet dogs. He's a beagle. He's wearing a red collar. Answers to the name Rex. And he loves hot dogs, so we thought maybe he'd come and eat a few here. . . ."

"So you think your hot dog came for a hot dog?" the vendor cracked. He thought for a moment. "Hmmmm. We get lots of visitors on the boardwalk, as you can see. I am sorry but I see a lot of dogs here; it's hard to tell them apart. . . ."

I was trying to listen to every word Frank said, but I was a little distracted by the hot dogs in his hands. I licked my chops and hoped that maybe one of them would drop.

Off in the distance, a dog barked.

Rex? It sounded like him! I turned. Annie turned. We all pricked up our ears as the barking got closer. But the dog that raced past us was white and fuzzy, dragging a deflated beach ball in its mouth.

It wasn't Rex.

By now, the heat was getting to all of us. I was starting to feel a little dizzy and needed another drink of cool water. The boardwalk had no shade, and the hot ball of sun was rising even higher up in the sky.

"What now?" Annie asked.

"Plan B," James said.

"Which is?" Annie asked.

"Back to the drawing board?" James suggested.

I sniffed at the air again. What was a drawing board? I didn't know where we were headed next, but I hoped that I could pick up Rex's scent there, too.

Annie frowned. She worried that Rex had gone off with another family—or gotten pulled out by the tide.

"How about Plan H?" Annie suggested.

"Why H?" James asked.

Edward let out a laugh. "*H* for Hot Dog?!" he

said. Then he reached into his pocket and pulled out a few bills. "I know we need to hurry and find Rex," he said, "but I think you two need a little energy boost—in the form of a hot dog."

Frank, the vendor, was nice; he gave us two-for-one hot dogs.

Annie got hers with extra relish, while James ate his with lots of mustard. Annie tossed me a bite. Yum!

After the eats, we'd only walked a few feet when I heard a loud "HOLD ON THERE, KIDS!" We turned back to the cart.

Frank waved his tongs at us. He'd remembered something else! At last! I let out a howl.

This royal hot doggy couldn't wait to find out what Frank had to say.

# Chapter 7

Frank dropped his tongs back into the vat of hot-dog water and wiped his hands on his apron. "Now I remember!"

Annie and James both smiled.

"I remember your dog! He *was* here. A little whippersnapper of a mutt!"

"Well," James grumbled, "he *is* a royal dog. And he's a purebred beagle, not a mutt. . . ."

"What happened is that a lady complained because your puppy jumped up and snatched her hot dog right out of the bun. With all this heat and the crowds, I'd nearly forgotten. . . ."

"Oh, that's good news!" James cheered.

Annie elbowed her brother in the side. "It's

good news that Rex swiped some woman's hot dog?"

James bit his lip. "Well, no . . . I mean . . ." For the first time, he looked worried and a little embarrassed. I think it was beginning to sink in: Rex was making trouble everywhere. Only, he had wandered too far away this time.

It wasn't cute anymore. It was scary! Rex might be in danger.

"Did you see where the beagle went after he ate the stolen hot dog?" Annie asked.

Frank stroked his chin in deep thought.

"Hmmm," he said. "I think your dog raced up the boardwalk there. Toward the aquarium. I remember, because we were all watching after he stole that woman's lunch. She was steamed."

Frank pointed a short distance away, toward the carnival section of the boardwalk. I raced off to find Rex among the games!

But Frank had one more thing to share.

"Hey, little dog!" he cried out as I darted off. I turned around just in time to see him hand something to Annie and James.

Annie winked at me and leaned down.

It was an *entire* hot dog! For me! I gulped it down in just two bites.

"Good, right, Sunny?" Annie said, giggling.

"Roowoorrooooo!" I howled.

"Keep an eye on the time," Edward reminded us. Nanny Sarah was waiting back on the beach.

James led the way toward the aquarium. Out in front was an enormous painted sign that read:

SHARK EXHIBIT. There was a gigantic photograph of a shark with a billion teeth, looking like he'd take a bite right out of me!

I got real low on the boardwalk and slunk along toward James.

"Hurry, Sunny!" Annie coaxed me.

Didn't she understand that sharks scared me?

All at once, I got a sniff of something interesting. A piece of hot-dog bun was just sitting there, in the middle of the boardwalk. People stepped around it. It looked half eaten.

I dived for it.

*Sniff, sniff, sniff.*

The bun smelled vaguely familiar! Ha! *Rex!*

Then I spotted some sand nearby. And the paw prints. Where had *those* come from? I sniffed again. Rex must have *just* been there. I spotted a construction sign that read: WET PAINT. He must have dodged in and out of the place where the boardwalk crew had painted the yellow lines. Messy dog!

I scooted toward the paint cans for another whiff, but the construction man waved me away.

"Get lost, mutt!" he cried. "You dogs! Another one of you just came through here and made a big mess!"

Annie and James heard that.

"REX!" they cried at the same time. The painted lines were on the way to the aquarium. At last, this was the evidence we needed. I saw even more traces of yellow paw prints as we walked along.

"Hurry up!" James bellowed. He was standing right in front of the shark sign. I ran over, panting. Was the sun getting hotter? I wished we were playing in the waves instead of searching for Rex.

Annie walked up to her brother. "Rex won't be in the aquarium," she said to James.

"How do you know that? Are you *psychic?*"

"No!" Annie said. She pointed to the main door. There was a sign on it that read: CLOSED WEDNESDAYS. It was a Wednesday.

"Oh," James said. "Well, let's keep going. . . ."

"Hey, kids!" Edward's booming voice nearly knocked me off my paws! I spun around.

Edward was shuffling behind us, dripping with sweat. His dark sunglasses had slipped to the very tip of his nose. "Where . . . are you . . . headed?" he asked breathlessly.

I eyed the sun in the white sky. What time *was* it?

Should we speak to the police who patrolled the

boardwalk? Let them know our dog was missing? I sniffed at the air and the ground some more. We really could not stop now after coming this far! I had this feeling we were close—*so* close.

If Rex had been here, and if he had walked past the aquarium without stopping . . .

"Hold on! I know where Rex went!" James blurted out.

"Huh? How do you suddenly know which way he went?" Annie said, imitating him. "Are you *psychic*?"

James made a face. "Oh, sure. Be that way. Fine!"

"James, this is *not* fine! Your dog is seriously lost—and we're running out of places to look for him!" Annie said.

"ROOOOOOOOOOOOOOOOOOOOOOW!"

I don't know what came over me, but I let out the loudest howl ever. Annie and James stopped talking and looked right at me. Edward laughed out loud.

"Gee, kids, I think maybe Sunny has something to tell us," he said.

"Wrrroooof!" I cried, tapping my paw on the ground as if to say, *Stop your bickering and follow me!*

If Nanny Sarah had been there, she would have said exactly that.

And then I, Sunny McDougal, rushed ahead. I followed the leftover yellow paw prints and the last of the hot-dog-bun crumbs. I sniffed the boardwalk until the Rex scent vanished.

Using puppy sense is the best—no, the *only*—way to get things done.

"Arrrrrf!" I stopped at last. The Rex scent led to an entranceway. Annie and James stopped short just behind me.

"Sunny?" Annie asked, bending down to pet my head again. "Is this where . . . ?"

I raised my eyes to meet Annie's and I nuzzled her hand.

"Rex is in here!" Annie cried. "Sunny to the rescue!"

We all looked up at the enormous, neon-lit gate. There was a sign blinking over our heads. I could read it by myself: HALL OF MIRRORS. People were lining up to get in. A large gray-haired woman was letting people in to the attraction. The sun was beating down like a laser beam on the spot where she stood. She did not look very happy. She was sweating more than Edward was.

It was so crowded! This must have been one of the most popular carnival attractions, next to the aquarium and Horrible House, the haunted maze. We'd already passed the aquarium, and Rex was not there. He would never have gone to some scary house with skeletons hanging outside. That would have been off limits for a scaredy-cat . . . er . . . scaredy-*pup*.

"Let's go!" James cried. "If Rex is in there, he's probably hungry and hot and who knows what else from all of his exploring!"

Hungry? Hot? I wanted to growl. That Rex had swiped a hot dog *and* who knows what else! If anyone was hot—under the collar—it was me. We'd spent most of the day looking for him! He always did whatever he wanted, and I was tired of it!

Thankfully, a cold rush of air-conditioning hit my fur as we went through the front door. If I needed to cool down, this was the place to do it.

# Chapter 8

It took a few minutes to get past the grumpy woman inside the door leading to the Hall of Mirrors. But Edward told the lady how Rex was a royal dog who needed to get back to the palace for a special ceremony.

"This beagle is the honored guest of the king and queen at Glimmer Rock palace," Edward explained. "He is to be awarded the highest medal of honor, the Royal Pooch Pin."

Annie and James giggled. It was mostly the truth, but it sounded funny the way Edward said it. "Royal dog? Step this way!" the woman said with a wide grin as she welcomed us through the turnstile. I darted underneath and felt a cold draft flow through a long tunnel.

*Aaaaaaaaah.*

It made me think of the feeling I'd had that morning on the tiled floor at the palace. My body temperature dipped and everything inside me calmed down.

It was so dark in there, but I didn't mind. Why wasn't every single person on the hot boardwalk spending the day in here?

"Sunny?"

Annie called my name. But I couldn't see her. It was darker in here than I had thought at first.

"Rowf?" I tried to bark softly. But it came out like *"ROWF!"*

That's because inside a hall of mirrors even the smallest sound echoes. The noise ricochets off every surface. By the time the echoes quieted, I wasn't sure *what* I was hearing. I heard footsteps. Then barks. Then sniffing. Then giggles. Then . . . Wait! *Sniffing?*

Hold on!

Was there another dog in there with us? If so, maybe that dog was Rex!

I listened closely, but I didn't hear any other

dog sounds, so I kept walking. Maybe those sniffs I was hearing really were just my imagination.

"Sunny? Sunny?" Annie said.

Each time Annie said my name, no matter how quietly she whispered, I heard it reverberate like freight trains running through the place.

Edward's voice was pretty loud, too, but the loudest person of the bunch was James. Because he was so eager to find Rex, he started *screaming* Rex's name when he entered the Hall of Mirrors. The loudness of his voice seemed to take even James himself by surprise.

Rex?

Rex?

Rex?

Wham! All at once, I hit a wall of rubber. But it moved, like the biggest doggy door ever. Now Annie was by my side again. We went into another space where the air-conditioning was blasting!

There was a flashing ball of light in this room, too.

Well, it wasn't actually a room, was it? It was a winding path through mirrors and glass. I'd never seen anything like it, not even in those doggy dreams of mine.

I kept walking, thinking Annie and Edward were behind me. Suddenly, Annie appeared in front of me! Then I saw James. But he wasn't really there, either. They were both reflections.

I didn't know where I was going.

*Where was I going?*

"ROWF?" I barked.

Right away I heard a shout back: "SUNNY!"

We kept shouting and barking, trying to find each other. This maze wound around like a coil. I had to find an exit. I wanted out of here! Why would anyone think this place was fun? I was lost and confused and . . .

"ROOWOOOOOWOOWOF!"

What had Rex thought as he raced inside

this place, looking for someone to play with?

*Annie? Where are you?*

"Sunny!" Annie gushed, appearing at last in front of me. She scooped me up. She lifted me in her arms and smothered me with kisses. "Oh, Sunny, I was so afraid! I didn't want to lose you! Two dogs lost in one day would be too much!"

I licked Annie's face. It tasted like salt and sunblock—not the best flavors. But I kept licking. I wished for a moment that we were back at the palace, until I remembered how hot it was there. Maybe it was better being right here, with the princess that I loved.

This whole beach adventure was definitely *not* how I remembered it from my earlier doggy days.

"WWWWWAAAAAOOOOOF!"

Annie looked at me.

"Was that you?" she asked.

I had not made that noise.

"Was that Rex?" Annie asked. She called out for James, but he didn't answer. Then she put me back down on the ground.

"Follow me!" she said.

I stayed right at her heels as we continued quickly through the maze. Where had James and

Edward gone? Somehow, we'd become separated. This wasn't a good thing.

Every time I started to walk through a part of the maze, I had to stop. There was always a wall of glass in the way! One path led to a dead end. Another looked like it went on and on for a mile. There must have been a real way out of there.

I sniffed along the floor: stale cotton candy, sneakers, and dirt. But I didn't smell our beagle. No Rex anywhere. No palace smell.

Where had that dog disappeared to now?

Annie called me over to a doorway. There was a bright light pointing the way to an outdoor space. I blinked at the brightness, hoping this would lead somewhere important. What was the source of that strange bark we'd heard? Was it out here?

We walked from the air-conditioned area through another black rubber door onto an enclosed balcony that looked out over the whole beach. Here was a glass wall that showed the entire boardwalk and coastline from above. It was an amazing view. I missed that puppy more than ever. I realized this whole place would have been way more fun with Rex by my side in the darkness of the Hall of Mirrors, and out here, overlooking the park.

I stuck my snout right up against the glass and looked out as far as I could look. Where was the palace from here? How many people were walking around down there?

"Whatcha looking at?" Annie asked me. "Ruff!" I barked. It sounded a little like Rex. Annie nodded. "Me, too," she said.

I was so glad that my princess was right there with me. I wondered if Rex was nervous without his prince.

Annie crouched down by my side and looked around. "This place is huge. Did you see the mirrors along the walls here? That one makes me look as skinny as a shoestring french fry!"

The two of us went up to each mirror to see what illusion it would show. Some made me appear flat, as if I had no legs, while Annie's legs looked half their size. Some made me look like a goldendoodle balloon that someone was about to pop, and some inflated Annie's head into an extra-large watermelon.

A crowd of kids came pushing through after us.

Edward and James eventually came through the door, too.

"Thank goodness you're here!" James cried,

sounding more worried than ever. "Did you find Rex? Did you see anything? Did you hear anything?"

I shook my head sadly. "*Ruff,*" I barked quietly.

"We didn't see another little doggy anywhere," Annie said. "We did, however, hear this strange bark. Maybe that *could* have been Rex...."

Up on the walls of the outside balcony was a row of terrific old carnival posters. I loved the pictures.

## BEAR MAN—ALIVE!

I wondered what a bear man *was*. A guy who needed a haircut?

## TWO-HEADED TORTOISE

What could be stranger, I wondered, than a turtle

with two heads? That just sounded kind of gross.

## UNIQUE MONIQUE

The woman painted on that sign had lost her head.

Then there was the best sign of all:

## FREE POPCORN

*Mmmmmmmm. Popcorn.*

I'd eaten a hot dog, but a snack sounded good. Gee, now who was getting distracted? We had to find Rex. This was no time for snacks.

"Come along, Sunny," Annie said. "We should go back and tell Nanny Sarah what we discovered. Maybe we'll find police on the boardwalk."

Edward let out a cough. "Wait, children!" he cried. "Down there! Look! Isn't that . . ."

"R-E-E-E-E-E-E-E-EX!"

James banged on the window for a moment, until Annie made him stop. Down below us, on the boardwalk, we saw Rex, scampering along with his tail held high. That beagle looked like he didn't have a care in the world.

"How did he get down there?" Annie asked.

"Maybe he wasn't ever up here!" James said, the truth finally dawning on him. "We'd better hurry if we're going to catch him, though—once and for all. Let's go!"

I wanted to collapse on the ground. That puppy was trotting along downstairs chasing strangers, but this puppy was in no mood to do any more chasing.

The view was much nicer than my view on the boardwalk of hundreds of legs and feet. I could see *everything* from here. But to get to Rex, we had to move. Edward led the way.

Oh, I hated to leave the air-conditioning! As we walked through the door marked EXIT ONLY, I nearly choked on the summer air outside. I wished I could just take off my fur coat.

I needed a cool swim!

James raced down the boardwalk in the direction he thought he'd seen Rex headed.

I set my nose to sniffing.

Right away I picked up a fresh scent.

It definitely smelled like beagle!

# Chapter 9

My nose went to work. Mixed in with Rex's scent, I smelled sand and hot dog and the floor of the House of Mirrors—all the places where we'd been chasing that dog today. The scents led me, Annie, James, and Edward to a shop that was located a few yards back from the boardwalk.

# CANDY LAND

I perked up right away. Candy! Here? I couldn't believe our luck. Rex had to be inside this shop! My nose knew!

*Brinngg-a-lingy-ling.*

The silver bell hanging on the glass door to the

candy shop tinkled when Edward pulled the door wide open.

Luckily for us, this place was air-conditioned, too, just like the House of Mirrors. A cold whoosh of air hit us when we walked inside.

This rowdy bunch of kids in bathing suits and towels stood at one counter. They were pointing at the wall. There must have been a hundred bins filled with candy in all shapes and sizes. That was definitely something to get excited about.

Even from where I stood, down on the floor, I could see green gum balls and red jelly beans up there, staring down at me. I could almost hear the candy whispering, *Eat me! Eat me!*

Drool slid out of the corners of my mouth. Of course, I was also still panting heavily because of the heat outside.

Wow! Was that really an entire shelf of chocolate bars in different sizes, with flower-shaped gummy candies, malted-milk balls, and peanut brittle, too?

Kids yelled out their orders to the shop owner.

Rex had to be here. That palace puppy always found the sweets in the pantry back at McDougal Palace. He had probably sniffed his way around the boardwalk until he found this shop. He might have been hiding and waiting to pounce on me, with cherry-licorice shoelaces in his mouth. . . .

"Grrrrrrrrrrrrrrrrowf!"

A dog barked! The sound came from behind a row of shelves. Rex?

I peeked around a corner display. A cocker spaniel was chewing on a rawhide shoe. Her fur had been tied with bows on the top of her head. So fancy! If only I had fur that could be tied up in bows.

"Who are you?" I asked the spaniel.

"Who are *you*?" the dog asked me as I approached.

I wagged my tail. "I'm Sunny. I'm just a visiting dog. Do you belong to the shop?"

The spaniel jumped up and licked her lips. "I do. Do you belong to someone?"

"I do," I replied. "I belong to Princess Annie."

"Oh! A princess?" the spaniel panted. "You're a royal pup. Figures I'd meet two of you in one day."

"Two?" I blurted out. "You met *another* royal pup?"

"Oh, yes. Another palace puppy was just in

the shop a little while ago, begging for something sweet. He was so crazy!"

"A *crazy* palace puppy?" I barked.

"Shhhhh," the spaniel said, wincing at the sound of my voice. "If you bark too loud, the candy jars will shatter!"

I spun around, expecting to find Rex close by, chewing on a gumdrop. Oh, how that beagle was going to get it!

But Rex wasn't nearby.

"The puppy left the shop," the spaniel said, sighing.

"Where did he go?" I asked.

The spaniel looked to the front door and then to the back of the shop. She looked back at me and wagged her tail.

"Out the front door," she said. "To the playground, I think. I told him there were sprinklers down there."

Sprinklers?

What a perfect place for a hot dog—and not the kind of hot dog that goes in a bun!

My collar jangled, and I headed to the door. Rex had been here—and now he was gone again? This was too much!

From across the store, Annie called to me.

"Sunny!" she cried. "Did you find Rex?"

I wanted to introduce her to the shop spaniel, but when I turned around, the spaniel had gone.

Annie held out a stick. It was a beefy chew stick! Hoorah! I bit into it with happiness. Turns out that Candy Land had another special shelf of dog treats: candy made just for pups like me.

All this puppy-searching had made me seriously hungry.

"Time to hit the road," James said as he walked toward us. "The shop owner just told me the only dog in this place is *her* dog."

I chewed up the beefy stick and looked at Annie for another treat.

Annie and James bought pops and suckers and chocolate and all sorts of fruit chews: raspberry, lemon, peach, and even banana. I wanted to try everything. Of course, dogs can't really eat chocolate, because it makes us sick. But I was ready to try all the other stuff!

*Rrrrrruff!*

"I don't know where to look for Rex now," Annie said.

I barked at her as if to say, *I do know! Let's go!*

*Rex is right over there* playing *in sprinklers while we stand here worrying!*

"Kids, it's getting late," Edward announced. He didn't know I was leading them in the right direction again. He wanted to turn back to Nanny Sarah? No!

I barked and zoomed ahead so they'd follow me.

"Sunny!" Annie cried out. "Stop, Sunny! Please don't run!"

But I was off.

A few moments later, we reached the sprinkler park behind the boardwalk. It was, as I had expected, *packed*.

I sniffed again. All I could smell was hot, wet kids. And I could see them screaming and splashing.

I got sprayed by one of the jets of water from minifountains as it spurted up from the ground.

I loved getting wet, of course. Getting wet and cool!

"Do you think Rex is here?" Annie asked me, frantically looking around the place. "Do you think he came here to cool off?"

James started looking around, too.

But after a long scavenger hunt through the fountains, the four of us came up empty. Even Edward was out of ideas. That spaniel from the shop had given me the wrong information.

James sat down on a nearby bench and put his head in his hands.

I knew he was upset. His face was all wet, and it wasn't from the sprinklers.

Annie took the wrapper off a Blue Raspberry lollipop and handed it to her brother. That was his favorite flavor pop—the kind that made his lips turn purple-blue.

James kicked a rock on the ground and stared at the pavement. I pawed my way over and nuzzled his leg a little with my snout.

At first, James ignored me. So I knocked into his leg a little bit harder.

"Oh, Sunny," Annie said. "I don't think James feels like . . ."

All at once I leaped right up into James's lap. He embraced my puppy body and I squeezed against him. I was a little big, but he held on. He needed a hug.

James started to cry. I'd never heard him do that before.

"Rex is gone, isn't he?" James said to his sister. "It's all my fault."

Edward put his hand on James's shoulder.

"We've only just begun our search for your dog," he said. "We still need to contact the boardwalk security team, put up flyers with Rex's picture, and look some more. We won't give up. Right, Annie? Right, Sunny?"

"ROWWWWWWWF!" I barked and jumped off James's lap.

The crowds at the sprinklers were thinning out. I trotted over to a water spout and ducked underneath.

*Aaaaaaaaah.*

"What are you doing?" someone asked me.

I poked my head back out of the stream of water and nearly fell over.

"REX!" I yelped.

Annie must have heard me bark out loud; or maybe she had seen Rex, too. She and James came racing over.

Rex was stretched out under an enormous spouting sprinkler, with his paws crossed and his eyes closed. That beagle looked like he did not have a care in all the world.

James scooped up his puppy and held him at arm's length.

"Where have you been!?" James scolded Rex. Then he grabbed him close. "I was so worried, you silly puppy."

I wanted to tell Rex that he'd actually made James *cry*.

But I didn't want to ruin the mood, so I kept it to myself.

"You're a bad dog," I said to Rex as we headed back—finally—to our towels, our chairs, and Nanny Sarah. "We were looking for you all day long. Do you know that? Why did you have to run away? Do you understand how serious this was?"

"Oh," Rex said. He looked at me like I had three tails. "I didn't know," he said. "I was just . . . um . . . curious. Did you have lunch yet? All I had was a hot dog on the boardwalk. Well, and some other snacks along the way. Did you know they have entire shops that sell only cotton candy? Did you also know that the people who are at the beach like to feed you when you're dashing around?"

I raced ahead.

That beagle was more frustrating than a fly in my doggy dish.

I knew Nanny Sarah would give us a snack right away once we returned to our tent and towels on the beach. I told Rex just to keep his snout shut until then. He was in enough trouble already.

After treats and some water, I'd get back to my sand and surf.

For once, I could stop worrying about Rex!

# Chapter 10

"You found him!" Nanny Sarah cheered as we came into view. We were hot and tired after our long search. I felt like our paws and feet were just barely shuffling along.

Rex, on the other hand, was racing back to our tent.

He barked nonstop as we headed toward Nanny Sarah on the beach. He kicked sand up on every towel he passed.

Not again!

As soon as he got to our red umbrella, Rex went right over and licked Nanny Sarah's knees. He danced some kind of doggy jig. Of course, that only kicked up more sand! Nanny Sarah didn't seem upset. She leaned down and stroked the top of Rex's head.

"We were so worried!" she exclaimed. "You can't go running off like that, young puppy. Do you understand?"

Rex nodded.

Oh, sure. *Now* he was being a good dog.

Of course, Nanny Sarah went on, she wasn't only worried about Rex. She had been worried about all of us. "You were gone for so long I didn't know what to think!" she explained.

"Here, Nanny Sarah," James said, extending his hand. He held out a lollipop and some licorice. "We got these for you. We were thinking about you the whole time, too."

"Oh, no candy for me," she replied. "It's too hot, don't you think? I've been sitting here sweltering while you four were off on a sugary adventure. . . ."

Then she gave me a look.

"Were you eating candy, too, Sunny?" she asked.

I wagged my tail between my legs as she leaned down to inspect my teeth. She always does that back at the palace.

"Well, I see something that looks a little bit like jelly bean, but otherwise, you look perfect,"

Nanny Sarah said, smiling. "Thanks, Sunny, for your extra help today."

Fortunately for us, the crowd on the beach had begun to thin out a little bit.

We all gathered on the towels and gazed up at the blue sky for a little while. I counted seagulls. Rex jumped up to count them, too—on the run—but James dragged him right back.

"You need to behave!" James yelled. He was still upset about Rex's running away.

Rex stopped in his tracks and cocked his head to one side.

And for the very first time that I can remember, I think he listened. He looked up at his prince and saw how James was feeling.

And Rex was clearly sorry.

"Arf!" I barked at him as he settled back onto the towel next to mine. "Why do you run away? How many times are you going to do that?" I asked him.

Rex looked at me, panting. "I don't know why I do it," he said. "But I'll try hard not to. I promise I will."

I smiled at him.

Our food from the red cooler had been worth

waiting for. We licked our chops—and licked our doggy bowls when it was served: chicken-liver kibble, I think, with some cut-up vegetables and a rawhide nugget for dessert. It wasn't the palace-people food I'd hoped for, but it filled my tummy and made me sleepy.

I think Rex and I both fell asleep for a short while after lunch. When I awoke, Rex was actually having a doggy dream. I saw his paws moving as if he were swimming in the ocean.

That, of course, gave me an idea.

Annie and James had run down to the water's edge, to build a sand castle and dance in the surf. Up where we were, Nanny Sarah had her nose in a book. She would read a page and then look up to check on the prince and princess—and on us, too, of course. Especially Runaway Rex.

I poked Rex in the ears and he awoke with a start.

"Hey!" Rex woofed. "Whatcha do that for?"

I leaned over and whispered to him, "Follow me. I have a plan."

"Oh, no," Rex replied. "I'm not following anyone. I don't want to get into trouble again. I know I'm already going to be punished when we get back to the palace. I don't want it to be worse than it already is!"

"You won't get punished!" I promised.

I darted off the towel where I'd been lying and gently took the blue boogie board in my mouth.

Rex's eyes lit up. "No, no," he said.

I blinked a few times and dropped the board at his paws. "Pretty please?" I asked.

"Go ahead, Rex!" Nanny Sarah said. She nodded her approval. "But be careful, you two! Don't hit anybody on the way to the water!"

Rex quickly took his board up and ran off. I followed eagerly. I showed Rex how to carry the board safely and carefully so he wouldn't get teeth marks on it.

Together, we made our way down to the ocean's edge. Annie and James saw us coming with the blue—and pink—boogie boards in our mouths.

"Awesome!" James exclaimed as we neared the water.

Rex naturally dropped his board at Annie's feet the moment he saw a sandpiper on the beach. He'd rather chase birds than surf, I guess.

Annie picked the pink board up off the sand and put it under her arm.

I gave the blue board to James.

I could tell from the look on James's face that he expected Annie would argue with him again about which board she wanted to use. She'd been so sure earlier that she could only use the blue one.

"Don't even ask," James said. "I am not giving you this blue boogie board."

Annie chuckled. "Oh, yeah?"

"YEAH!" James said. He looked serious, too. He was not joking around.

"I'm not going to ask for the blue one," Annie said. "I'm going to try really hard not to argue at all."

James looked stunned. "Whoa," he said. "Who are you, and what have you done with my sister?"

Annie laughed again. So did I; I laughed one of those puppy laughs, as I had earlier in the day. Because I understood what they were saying. And I understood more than that, too.

It had started out as a crabby, hot day in the palace. Searching for Rex hadn't made the crabby parts any better.

But now, here we were, one happy family: me, Rex, Annie, and James. We were having our moment in the sun *and* water.

# PUPPY POWER

"REX!" James bellowed down the beach. There was that beagle, roaming the wrong way *again*.

But this time, Rex didn't argue. He romped right back to the rest of us and started digging in the sand.

"ROOOOWF!" I said, congratulating him. "You're a good boy, Rex," I added.

Rex looked at me and snarled. "I know I'm a good boy!"

I laughed again.

"Look!" Annie cried. "Up in the sky!"

We all craned our necks to read a message in the sky. A plane had left a trail of smoke behind it: PUPPY POWER.

James and Annie laughed when they read the message. It was the name of some cartoon show that they watched on television, but it was also the perfect message for today's wild adventure.

I playfully flicked a little sand over toward Rex. The temperature was cooler outside. The water felt refreshing! It was also cool just being there, together with my doggy friend.

No matter what else happened, I'd always be there for Rex, and he'd be there for me. Even if it meant sniffing my way around the beach boardwalk for an entire steaming day.

We stayed at Glimmer Rock Beach until the sun began to sink in the sky. As the red and yellow circle disappeared below the horizon, Rex wagged his tail against mine.

"Know what, Sunny?" Rex said. "You're my best friend. Thanks for always looking out for me!"

I smiled. "That's just my puppy power!" I quipped.

Rex barked out loud in agreement. Then we both took off for the edge of the water and ran playfully into the oncoming surf.

Keep reading for a sneak peak
at the next book in the
Palace Puppies series:

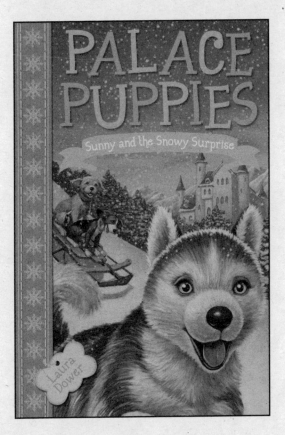

# Chapter 1

"Groowwwf!" Rex barked at me from the doorway to Princess Annie's bedroom.

He chased his tail all the way over to my doggy bed.

"Get up, Sunny!" Rex tugged at my blanket.

"Rex!" I grumbled, eyes still half closed. "What do you want?"

It usually takes a hundred-piece orchestra to wake me up in the morning. But not with Rex around. He wakes up and runs around before the sun rises. Rex is a beagle who just can't sit still. This morning, he must have been awakened by the blustery winds outside. Now that I was awake, I could hear them, too.

Rex and I live together at McDougal Palace in the kingdom of Glimmer Rock. Kings and queens aren't as common these days as they used to be, but I'm happy and proud to say that I belong to a modern royal family. My owner is Princess Annie. Rex belongs to Prince James. The McDougals have been the royal family of Glimmer Rock for centuries. We have our own coat of arms and everything!

"Come on, Sunny!" Rex pleaded. "I've never seen anything like this! You have to come look! Now!"

Rex stepped back for a moment, tail wagging. I could see him panting.

"Rex!" I growled. "Please get away from my bed."

"DON'T YOU WANT TO SEE THE SNOW?" Rex howled.

"Snow?" I hopped up and leaned into my morning stretch, paws pressed forward as I arched my back and yawned. *That sounded interesting.* My tail wagged a less grouchy good morning.

Rex barked. "Come downstairs! I want to show you!"

I shook my body hard. Oh, what a sleep it had

been! I'd dreamed that I was stranded on a dog-bone-shaped desert island with an unending supply of Beefy Yums. Just thinking about them made me as hungry as a . . . well, as a puppy stranded on a desert island!

"Sunny!"

"I'm coming, Rex," I barked back. "I *have* seen snow before."

"You have never seen snow like this!" Rex growled as he led the way out of Annie's bedroom.

We both flew down the large center staircase, sniffing madly at the air. I had to see this special snow Rex was talking about.

The carpeting on the stairs smelled like sweet jasmine. And baby powder. And there was this bleach smell, too, that got stronger as I reached the bottom of the staircase.

Winter was tough on palace floors. The marble got scuffed by boots and spattered by mud. This time of year, the palace staff had more than usual to clean up.

Rex scooted around a bucket of soapy water and a mop that had been left smack in the middle of the entryway. The large, circular entryway to the palace had marble columns and oil paintings on every wall. There were even paintings of animals and flowers on the ceiling!

"See?" Rex indicated the enormous picture window a short distance away. "Look at all that snow!"

I stopped in my tracks.

Wow.

Rex was right. There was snow, snow, snow, everywhere!

I'd never seen or played in that much snow. It looked as if the palace chef had vanilla-frosted the entire property.

Yum!

We headed for the library. I smelled the fire in the oversize stone fireplace—one of eight in MacDougal Palace.